A Day
with AJ

First day of school

by Mabel Reyes

AuthorHouse™
1663 Liberty Drive
Bloomington, IN 47403
www.authorhouse.com
Phone: 1 (800) 839-8640

Published by AuthorHouse 02/14/2019

ISBN: 978-1-5462-7980-8 (sc)
ISBN: 978-1-5462-7979-2 (e)

Library of Congress Control Number: 2019901567

Print information available on the last page.

Any people depicted in stock imagery provided by Getty Images are models,
and such images are being used for illustrative purposes only.
Certain stock imagery © Getty Images.

This book is printed on acid-free paper.

Because of the dynamic nature of the Internet, any web addresses or links contained in this book may have changed
since publication and may no longer be valid. The views expressed in this work are solely those of the author and do not
necessarily reflect the views of the publisher, and the publisher hereby disclaims any responsibility for them.

authorHOUSE®

A Day with AJ

First day of school

Hi! My **name** is Aj. I am six years old and I have Down Syndrome. I have two older brothers. My mom is a nurse. My dad is a welder. We live in Texas!

name

Today is my first day of school. I get to ride the **bus**!

bus

I am a little scared, **but** I will be okay. I will have fun and make new friends.

but

That **is** my teacher, Mrs. Ross. We are learning our abc's.

It is lunchtime. **We** get in a straight line and keep our hands to ourselves. Today **we** are having pizza!

we

After lunch is recess. There are lots of **fun** activities to do on the playground!

fun

Mrs. Ross reads a story before we go home. We must **be** careful listeners while she reads.

be

It is time to go **home**! It was a fun day!

home

Going to school was not so scary. I made friends **and** learned a lot. I learned to keep my hands to myself. I learned to listen carefully. I learned that school was fun.

and

See **you** all tomorrow!

YOU

Printed in the United States
By Bookmasters